First published in the United States of America in 2020 by Chronicle Books LLC.

Originally published in Japan in 2016 under the title *Natsumi wa Nannidemo Nareru* by PHP Institute, Inc. English translation rights arranged with PHP Institute, Inc. through Rico Komanoya.

Library of Congress Cataloging-in-Publication Data available.

ISBN 978-1-4521-8038-0

Manufactured in China.

Typeset in Minou.

10 9 8 7 6 5 4 3 2 1

Chronicle Books LLC
680 Second Street
San Francisco, California 94107

Chronicle Books—we see things differently.
Become part of our community at www.chroniclekids.com

I CAN BE ANYTHING

Shinsuke Yoshitake

chronicle books · san francisco

No, it isn't.

It's a pot!

It's very easy.

First question:
What is it?

Let's see. Something dancing?

Next, what is this?

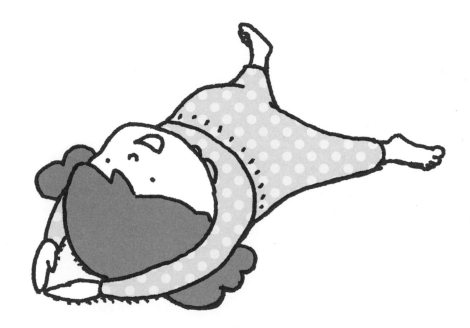

Well . . . is it an arrow sign?

No, it isn't.

It's a clothespin!

Next, what is this?

 Is it a doll?

No, it isn't.

It's a rice ball!

Next, what is this?

 A caterpillar?

No, it isn't.

It's an omelet!

Next, what is this?

A pointy omelet?

It's Mount Fuji!

Excuse me, but I need
to fold the laundry now.

Would you like to
finish the game
with three more?

OK, ten more!

What is this?

 Washing your face?

No, it isn't.

It's Santa Claus!

What is this?

I don't know.

It's shellfish in miso soup!

Next, what is this?

 An upside-down bug?

No, it isn't.

It's a baby!

What is this?

Shhh

Shhh

Shhh

 Wait! Don't do that!

It's a bulldozer!

Next, what is this?

 I have no idea.

It's an electric fan!

What is this?

This?

This?

This?

This?

This?

And this?

I have no idea.

They're all kinds of aliens!

Wow.

OK. So, what is this?

 Um, taking a nap?

No, it isn't.

It's the over-cooked broccoli
you sometimes make.

Now, what is this?

Well . . .

It's me eating a lot of fried chicken!

Next, what is this?

 Is it feeling like crying?

No, it isn't!

It's the feeling of not wanting
to go to the dentist!

OK, then can you understand *this* game?
It's the "Where am I?" game.

Now, what is this?

I don't know.

It's a mom peeling the
skin off of her foot.

I see. Can you please pretend
to be something other than me?

Sure. What is this?

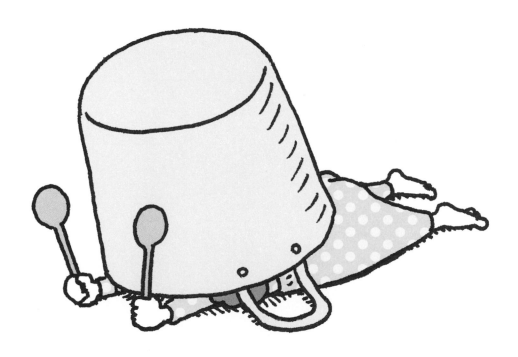

 I really don't know. Give me a hint.

Hello?

Natsumi?

Wow, you're asleep!

Zzzzz